The Little RedMill

The Little Red Mill

By Bob L. Bradley

Boo...Hoo...Cried the little red mill as he sat beside the happy little stream. The little stream bubbled and gurgled but he could not make the little red mill smile. You see, the little red mill was unhappy because he was lonesome. Try as he may, he could not make himself content to sit alone by the small stream.

He had at one time been a busy little mill. He'd been delighted with all of his activity. Farmers came with their children in their wagons filled with grain to be ground. Merchants came to buy flour for their stores. This made the little mill happy because he liked people and wanted to have them coming and going through his little red door.

But now no one ever came to see him. His visitors were the mice, who came to build their nests in the comers of his storage room Sometimes the squirrels played in and out of his broken windows. The closest he ever got to people was to catch sight of them as they sped by along the turnpike that had been built near to his front door. He would wiggle his paddle wheel or flap a shutter when they passed. He hoped to get someone to stop and say hello. They just went swishing by, not even noticing the poor little mill weeping into the nearby stream.

Then one day a big shiny car turned off from the turnpike and came in his direction. The little mill was so happy that he flapped his paddle wheel three times. The car stopped in front of the mill and a big, important-looking man got out. He looked the little mill over from one end to the other. Tapped on the walls, pounded on his beams, chiseled at his foundation until the little mill began to ache, but because he was so happy he really didn't mind at all.

Finally he seemed to be satisfied because he quit pounding and took from his car a large sign. The only words that the little mill could read before the man nailed it to his front door was two big red words, ''For Sale!''

Then the little mill began to worry. Oh Dear, Oh Dear, what was to become of me now? He began to dread seeing that big car turn in his drive and head his way. People would get out and go through his rooms from top to bottom He was stomped, kicked, hammered, chipped, scraped, and beaten upon until he thought his poor walls could not stand it any longer. But always the people shook their heads and said, "No, it's not quite what we want," or ''It would cost too much to tear it down and build again." All this made the little mill more sad than ever. No one seemed to think he was worth anything and no one wanted him.

Nothing happened for several weeks and the little mill worried and worried, ''What will they do with me now?" Then one day a man came with pencil and paper and went from room to room drawing pictures. He looked all over the ground around the little mill and then drove away.

One day as he was feeling particularly blue and lonely, the big car turned in and stopped. The big important man brought along with him a happy couple, who looked all around the little mill. The little mill could tell by the way they walked from room to room talking that they were nice people. They didn't even bang once on his walls or scrape at his foundation. They stayed for a long time. When they were ready to leave, the real estate man took down the big sign. The little mill began to feel happy because at last he was going to belong to someone. Yet, what were they going to do with him?

One day in early May things began to happen. First came the carpenters. They hammered and sawed. They hung windows and doors. They built new walls and laid new floors. Some of those things were painful for the little mill, but he never groaned or complained once. He was happy that people were coming to see him again.

Then came painters, who gave him a new coat of red paint on the outside and all kinds of nice colors on the inside. Then came the electricians. They put in new electric lights for the old lanterns that used to hang on the walls. Plumbers came and added bright, shiny pipes. Men came with big machines, bigger than any he'd ever seen, and moved the dirt around the little stream. Then men planted flowers and trees all around. Last of all, came men with big trucks loaded with chairs and tables, stoves and refrigerators, just so many things he couldn't keep track of them. He said to himself this has to stop. I'm getting dizzy from all of this activity."

Then all work stopped. The little red mill was so bright and clean that he just shone all over. His little paddle was turning happily in the stream and the people who drove by all looked his way. Still, he didn't know what he was going to be. Then early one morning a truck came with a big sign to hang on the post out in front of the little mill. When he read that sign, he knew he was always going to be happy from then on. He'd have people coming and going all of the time...

the sign read,
Welcome to the
Little Red Mill Restaurant
Where Happy People
Meet to Eat!

Edwards Brothers Malloy
Thorofare, NJ USA
September 5, 2012